For Jaime
and the beautiful shining silence

— & —

For Donna McCarthy
who'll always be a part of the team

Copyright © 2018 by David Wiesner

All rights reserved. For information about permission to reproduce selections from this book,
write to trade.permissions@hmhco.com or to Permissions, Houghton Mifflin Harcourt Publishing Company,
3 Park Avenue, 19th Floor, New York, New York 10016.

Clarion Books is an imprint of Houghton Mifflin Harcourt Publishing Company. hmhco.com

The illustrations in this book were created in acrylic, gouache, and watercolor.
The text was set in Gotham and Gill Sans. Book design by Carol Goldenberg.

Library of Congress Cataloging-in-Publication Data is available.
ISBN 978-0-544-30902-9

Manufactured in China   SCP 10 9 8 7 6 5 4 3 2 1   4500691125

I GOT IT!

David Wiesner

CLARION BOOKS / HOUGHTON MIFFLIN HARCOURT · BOSTON · NEW YORK

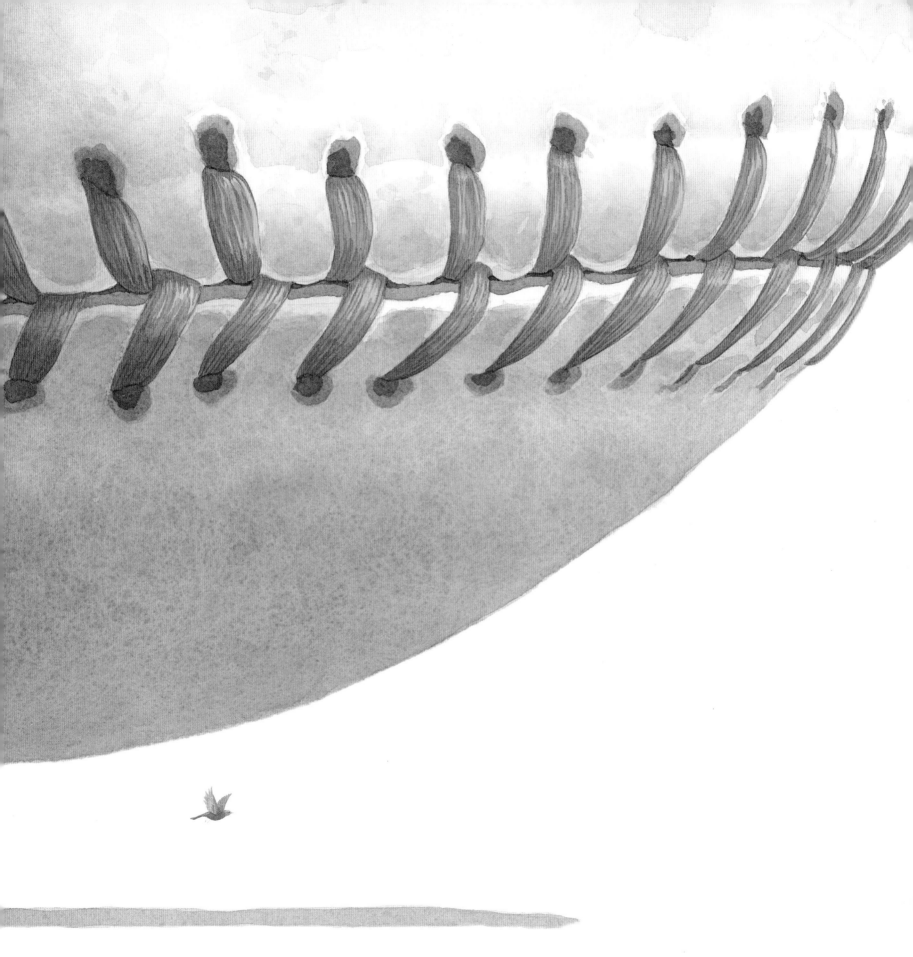